J
E   Stevenson, James, 1929-
Ste   Happy Valentine's Day, Emma! / by
       James Stevenson. -- 1st ed. -- New York
       : Greenwillow Books, c1987.
          [32] p. : col. ill. ; 21 x 26 cm.
          Summary: Despite Delores and
       Lavinia's nasty cards, Emma the witch
       and her friends have a wonderful
       Valentine's Day.
          ISBN 0-688-07357-3

          1. Valentine's Day--Fiction.
       2. Witches--Fiction. 3. Cartoons and
       comics. I. Title.

Happy Valentine's Day, Emma!

by James Stevenson

Greenwillow Books New York

Watercolor paints were combined
with pen drawings for the
full-color illustrations.

Library of Congress Cataloging-in-Publication Data
Stevenson, James (date)
Happy Valentine's Day, Emma!
Summary: Despite Dolores and Lavinia's
nasty cards, Emma the witch and her friends
have a wonderful Valentine's Day.
[1. Valentine's Day—Fiction.
2. Witches—Fiction.
3. Cartoons and comics]   I. Title.
PZ7.S84748Hap 1987   [E]   87-13
ISBN 0-688-07357-3
ISBN 0-688-07358-1 (lib. bdg.)